MW00748521

MISSION
FOX
ANIMAL RESCUE SERVICE

We rescue animals in danger
and find lost pets

Phone 040823590

FOR JACK, JULIETTE AND JAXON

PUFFIN BOOKS

Published by the Penguin Group
Penguin Group (Australia)
250 Camberwell Road, Camberwell, Victoria 3124, Australia
(a division of Pearson Australia Group Pty Ltd)
Penguin Group (USA) Inc.
375 Hudson Street, New York, New York 10014, USA
Penguin Group (Canada)
90 Eglinton Avenue East, Suite 700, Toronto, Canada ON M4P 2Y3
(a division of Pearson Penguin Canada Inc.)
Penguin Books Ltd
80 Strand, London WC2R 0RL England
Penguin Ireland
25 St Stephen's Green, Dublin 2, Ireland
(a division of Penguin Books Ltd)
Penguin Books India Pvt Ltd
11 Community Centre, Panchsheel Park, New Delhi – 110 017, India
Penguin Group (NZ)
67 Apollo Drive, Rosedale, Auckland 0632, New Zealand
(a division of Pearson New Zealand Ltd)
Penguin Books (South Africa) (Pty) Ltd
24 Sturdee Avenue, Rosebank, Johannesburg 2196, South Africa

Penguin Books Ltd, Registered Offices: 80 Strand, London, WC2R 0RL, England

First published by Penguin Group (Australia), 2011

3 5 7 9 10 8 6 4 2

Text copyright © Justin D'Ath, 2011
Illustrations copyright © Heath McKenzie, 2011

The moral rights of the author and illustrator have been asserted.

All rights reserved. Without limiting the rights under copyright reserved above,
no part of this publication may be reproduced, stored in or introduced into a retrieval
system, or transmitted, in any form or by any means (electronic, mechanical,
photocopying, recording or otherwise), without the prior written permission of both
the copyright owner and the above publisher of this book.

Cover, text and internal design by Evi O. © Penguin Group (Australia)
Colour separation by Splitting Image Colour Studio, Clayton, Victoria
Printed and bound in Australia by McPherson's Printing Group, Maryborough, Victoria
Typeset in ITC Officina Sans 12/22 pt by Post Pre-press Group, Brisbane, Queensland

National Library of Australia
Cataloguing-in-Publication data:

Snake escape / Justin D'Ath

978 0 14 330581 1

A823.3

puffin.com.au

JUSTIN D'ATH

MISSION FOX

SNAKE ESCAPE

with illustrations by HEATH McKENZIE

Puffin Books

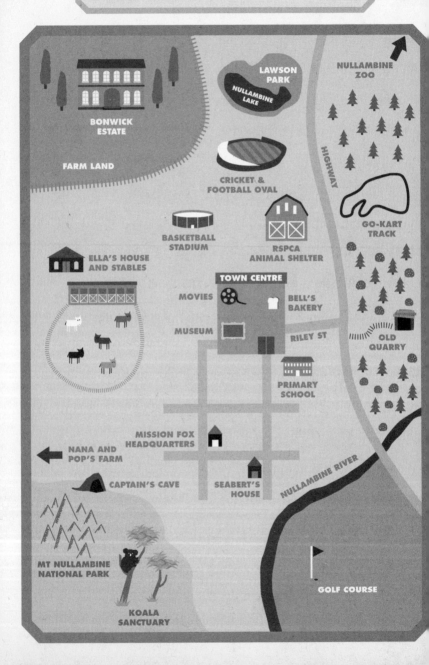

DO WE CATCH SNAKES?

Jordan Fox opened his eyes, feeling confused. It was Saturday. Why was he awake so early? And what was that noise?

Zzzz! Zzzz! Zzzz! Zzzz!

He lifted his head to listen. The noise was coming from across the room. It sounded muffled. Like an alarm clock covered with a blanket.

Or like a phone under a rock!

Jordan sat up and prodded the bunk above him.

'Harry, wake up!' he hissed. 'It's the FoxPhone!'

His twin brother made a grunting sound but didn't move. It always took Harry ages to wake up.

Jordan would have to answer the phone himself. **Gulp!**

He scrambled out of bed and crossed the room. On his desk there was a big glass tank with sticks and sand and rocks in it. The buzzing sound was coming from under one of the rocks. It was the perfect hiding place for a secret mobile phone. When the twins' mother cleaned their room, she *never* opened Max's tank.

Jordan had never opened it, either.

Until today.

Taking a deep breath, he slowly lifted the lid. Unlike his owner Harry, Max the tarantula was wide awake.

And he was sitting on the rock with the phone underneath!

Zzzz! Zzzz! Zzzz! Zzzz!

Jordan had to answer. People only rang the FoxPhone in an emergency.

He grabbed a ruler off the desk and carefully pushed the rock to one side. Max stayed on the rock. His eight beady eyes watched Jordan's trembling hand come slowly down and grab the phone away.

'Mission Fox Animal Rescue Service,' he whispered. 'Does an animal need help?'

'Well, I'm really the one who needs help,' said a shaky voice. It sounded like an old lady.

'I'm sorry,' Jordan told her. 'We only help animals, not people. Would you like me to call an ambulance or something?'

'Good heavens, no!' the old lady said. Jordan heard the sound of paper shuffling. 'I found this flyer in my letterbox, you see. It says you help find lost pets.'

Jordan knew the words on the flyer off by heart – they were *his* words. Well, Harry had helped a bit.

'Have you lost your pet?' Jordan asked.

'Well, Bella's my husband's pet, actually,' said the old lady. 'She's a snake.'

MISSION
FOX
ANIMAL RESCUE SERVICE

We rescue animals in danger
and find lost pets

Phone 040823590

A creepy feeling, like a tarantula's feet, ran up and down Jordan's spine.

Snakes freaked him out even more than giant hairy spiders. 'What sort of snake?' he asked nervously.

'A scrub python,' said the old lady.

'Hang on a minute,' Jordan said.

The FoxPhone had a special app called BRAIN (Bird, Reptile and Animal Identification Network). Jordan typed in *Scrub python* and a big scaly snake appeared on the screen. **Yikes!** Jordan nearly dropped the phone. Quickly he scrolled down to DESCRIPTION . It said scrub pythons were the largest snakes in Australia. They could grow to **eight metres** long!

Further down, under HABITS , was something even worse . . .

Jordan looked in the mirror, and made himself stand very tall.

He clicked the PHONE button.

'Is Bella a full-grown snake?' he asked.

'I don't know,' said the old lady. 'You'd have to ask my husband.'

'Can I talk to him, please?'

'That's the trouble, you see,' she said.

MAIN

DESCRIPTION

HABITS

ORIGIN

OTHER INFO

Scrub pythons eat possums, birds, wallabies and small kangaroos, and could be dangerous to small children.

Scrub Python _

Q W E R T Y U I O P 7 8 9
A S D F G H J K L del 4 5 6
Z X C V B N M < > / 1 2 3
aA @ space ! ? 0 .

BRAIN

'My husband's at the hospital. Yesterday my grandson came to visit and he must have left Bella's cage door open.'

'Do you know where Bella might have gone?' asked Jordan.

'I think she's somewhere in the house,' said the old lady. 'But I'm a bit scared to go looking for her.'

So was Jordan. 'Could you hang on again, please?' he asked.

Jordan crossed back to the bed, and gave his brother a big shake. 'Harry, do we catch snakes?'

'Uhhhhn,' went Harry.

Jordan waved the phone at him. 'Wake up! We've got a call on the FoxPhone.'

'Who is it?' Harry asked sleepily.

'An old lady,' whispered Jordan. 'She wants us to catch a snake.'

Suddenly Harry was wide awake. 'Awesome!' he cried. 'What sort of snake?'

Jordan told him about Bella.

Harry jumped down off his bunk and raced to the wardrobe to look at the handwritten chart that was taped to the back of the door.

'Our first Code Red mission!' he cried.

MISSION FOX
DANGER CODES

CODE BLUE	• budgies that won't go back into their cages • goldfish stuck in drains • baby animals that need help
CODE YELLOW	• lost or escaped pets that aren't goldfish or little birds or baby animals or snakes • pets and animals that are sick or hurt. *not snakes*
CODE RED	• wild animals that are sick or hurt • wild animals that are lost • scary animals that are sick or hurt or lost
CODE BRIGHT RED	• zoo break outs • crocodiles in people's swimming pools • poachers and bad guys doing mean stuff to animals

2

MISSION FOX TO THE RESCUE

Jordan wrote down the lady's name and address. She was called Mrs Seabert and she lived in the next street. Jordan got a fluttery feeling in his stomach when he thought about a huge, dangerous snake living just around the corner.

Now it was on the loose!

'Have you seen my T-shirt?' Harry asked when Jordan got off the phone.

'Look in the FoxPack,' Jordan whispered.

'I already did.'

The FoxPack was where they kept their

rescue equipment. Harry had tipped it out on the floor. Their Mission Fox uniforms lay on the carpet. They had matching green cargo shorts, Fox Sports baseball caps with the 'Sports' part blacked out, sunglasses and their special GoFaster runners. But there were no T-shirts.

'Mum must have washed them,' said Jordan.

He went to the wardrobe and pulled open the top drawer. Sure enough, both T-shirts were there – washed and neatly folded.

Jordan held one up to read the logo on the back.

AMINAL RESCUE, it said in big permanent-marker letters.

'Here's yours,' he whispered, tossing it to Harry, who wasn't very good at spelling.

The logo on the other T-shirt was spelt

FOXPACK

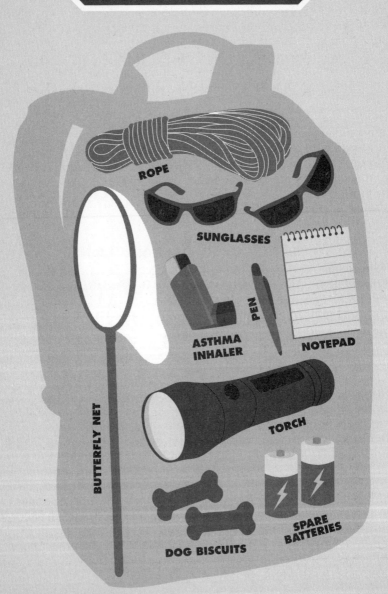

correctly: **ANIMAL RESCUE**. Jordan put it on.

'Will we take the FoxMobile?' Harry asked when they were dressed.

The FoxMobile was the three-wheeled billy cart they used on rescue missions.

Jordan shook his head. 'Mrs Seabert only lives around the corner,' he said. 'We'll just take Myrtle.'

After they had loaded all their rescue equipment into the FoxPack, the twins crept out and tiptoed downstairs to the lounge. It was very dark because the curtains were closed. Something huge and furry lay on a rug in front of the fireplace. It looked like a sleeping grizzly bear.

'Myrtle!' Jordan whispered.

The huge furry thing jumped up. It came bounding across the room and nearly bowled the boys over.

'Calm down, Agent M!' giggled Harry, as Myrtle wished them both a sloppy good morning.

Myrtle (or Agent M) was the third member of Mission Fox. She was a dog – a HUGE one. Part Great Dane and part Newfoundland, Myrtle was big enough to be in the *Guinness Book of Records*. She was the biggest dog in Australia. People often thought she was a pony. But animals didn't make that mistake. They knew what Myrtle was straight away. It sometimes caused problems when Mission Fox was supposed to rescue cats.

Jordan clipped on her lead and took her to the front door. Harry followed with the FoxPack. They had to be really quiet. Everyone else was still in bed.

Jordan and Harry's parents didn't know that Mission Fox was real. They thought it was just a made-up game the twins played. But Jordan and Harry wanted them to think that. No way would Mr and Mrs Fox let their two youngest sons go on dangerous rescue missions if they knew the truth.

It wasn't fair. The twins' older brother, Sam, was allowed to travel all around the world having amazing adventures, and their parents were proud of *him*!

Half a minute later, the three Mission Fox agents were safely outside. Nobody had heard them. The street was empty.

'Mission Fox to the rescue!' whispered Harry.

They gave each other the secret MF handshake.

'Woof!' went Myrtle, really quietly for such a big dog.

Jordan and Harry gave her the secret MF head-pat.

3

HISSSS!

Mrs Seabert was standing on her front porch looking up and down the street. She blinked in surprise when the three Mission Fox agents came walking up her path.

'Goodness me!' she said.

Adults often said things like that when they met the twins. It was because Jordan and Harry were identical, and Myrtle was so big.

'We're from Mission Fox,' Jordan said. 'You called us about the snake that escaped.'

'But you're just boys!'

'We're small for our age,' said Harry. He made his voice go deeper. 'Actually, we're nearly twenty.'

It wasn't a lie. The twins were nearly twenty if you added their ages together.

Mrs Seabert pointed at Myrtle. 'Is that a pony?' she asked.

Jordan shook his head. 'Myrtle's a dog.'

'Where's the snake?' asked Harry.

'I'm not really sure,' Mrs Seabert said nervously. She stepped to one side and pushed open her front door. 'Would you like to go in and see if you can find her?'

Harry went straight in. He was braver when it came to snakes. Jordan stayed outside with Myrtle and Mrs Seabert.

'Agent J!' Harry's voice came from inside. 'Aren't you going to help?'

Agent J was Jordan's code name. Jordan

and Harry needed to keep their real names secret in case someone told their parents.

'Is it all right if our dog comes in?' Jordan asked Mrs Seabert.

'Be my guest,' she said.

Jordan pointed at the open door. 'Find the snake, Agent M!'

Myrtle was good at sniffing things out. She ran into Mrs Seabert's house with her nose to the floor. Jordan stumbled in after her, hanging onto her lead. She dragged him down a short hallway and turned right, into a very dark room.

Then she started barking.

Jordan tried to hold her back. She was nearly pulling his arms off. Jordan took off his sunglasses and looked round the room. All he could see were the black shapes of furniture. Bella could be anywhere! It was the worst feeling. Jordan really wanted to switch on the light, but Myrtle was pulling so hard he couldn't let go to reach it. She was barking like crazy.

There was another noise, too: **_Hissss! Hissss! Hissss!_**

'Agent H!' yelled Jordan. 'I think Myrtle's found it!'

A Harry-shaped shadow appeared in the doorway. The light clicked on.

Now Jordan could see that he was standing in the middle of an old-fashioned lounge room. It was crowded with furniture that looked like it should be in a museum. Sitting on the back of a large flowery armchair was a hissing black cat.

Oops! thought Jordan. He'd forgotten to ask Mrs Seabert if she had a cat.

Myrtle didn't hate cats, she just liked chasing them. Now that the light was on, she could see the one she'd sniffed out.

With a deep, happy bark, she jumped at
the cat, ripping the lead out of Jordan's
hands.

The chase was on!

The cat let out a yowl of fright and
jumped off the back of the chair. It hit

the floor running. It shot under a little table with a lamp on it. It went skidding around the back of a couch. It ducked under another chair. And then it flew out the door between Harry's legs. All in about two seconds.

Myrtle wasn't far behind. The first chair toppled over. The little table went flying. The lamp crashed to the floor. The couch spun in a circle. The second chair tipped onto its side.

Harry got bowled over.

'Why did you let her go?' he asked, as Jordan helped him up.

'I didn't let her go!' Jordan said crossly. 'She got away.'

'I thought you could control her.'

'I can – except when she goes off chasing cats.'

They stopped arguing when they heard a crash and a loud **SCREEEECH** from one of the other rooms.

'Oops!' said Jordan.

'Follow me,' said Harry.

4

SHISHKEBAB!

They found Myrtle in the kitchen. The cat was there, too. It was crouched on top of the fridge, looking scared. Myrtle was sitting in front of the fridge, looking pleased with herself.

The cat was trapped. Myrtle had done her job.

But she'd made quite a mess of the kitchen. All sorts of things had been knocked over, including a big birdcage with a cockatoo in it. Mr and Mrs Seabert had lots of pets.

Including a snake, Jordan remembered as he grabbed Myrtle's lead.

Well, they would worry about that later. First they had to clean up the kitchen.

'Sit!' he told Myrtle. Then he helped Harry lift up the cockatoo's cage.

The cage was on a tall wooden stand. Harry pushed and Jordan pulled while the big white cockatoo flapped around inside in a panic.

Suddenly the cage door fell open and the cockatoo flew out!

It circled the kitchen a couple of times, then landed on the old-fashioned light high above the boys' heads.

'*WHO'S A PRETTY BOY?*' it shrieked.

'Quick! We'd better catch it before Mrs Seabert finds out,' said Harry.

Too late.

'What on earth are you doing?' the old

lady asked from the kitchen doorway.

'Your cockatoo got out,' Jordan said.

'I can see that,' said Mrs Seabert. She raised a bent old finger for the bird to land on. 'Come here, Charlie,' she said.

But Charlie took no notice. He wasn't looking at Mrs Seabert and he wasn't looking at Jordan and Harry. Or at Myrtle, or the cat. He was looking at the cupboards above the sink.

The twins looked up too.

'*Shishkebab*!' they gasped.

5

THINK LIKE A COCKATOO

Bella was enormous. She looked like one of the huge ropes they use to tie up ships. Except ships' ropes aren't covered in leathery scales. And they aren't alive.

Somehow, the monster snake had climbed up onto the cupboards above the sink. Her long, fat body was coiled in the little space between the cupboards and the ceiling. She was looking at Charlie, and Charlie was looking at her.

'Do Bella and Charlie like each other?' Harry asked Mrs Seabert.

'I don't think they've ever met.'

Jordan remembered something. 'On BRAIN it says that scrub pythons *eat* birds,' he said.

It looked like BRAIN was right. Bella had started to move towards Charlie. And there was a hungry look in her eyes. Slowly she stretched her head and neck across the gap between the cupboards and the swaying light.

Charlie just watched her getting closer.

Fly away! Jordan thought, but Charlie didn't move.

He was frozen in fear. In thirty seconds he would be Bella's breakfast.

'Please do something!' wailed Mrs Seabert. She sounded as scared as Charlie looked.

She sounded as scared as Jordan felt.

But Harry wasn't scared. Quickly he

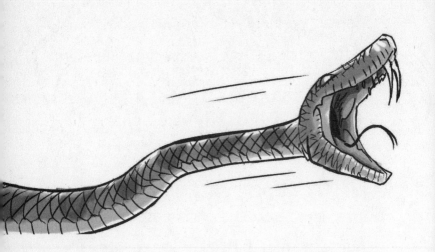

freed his arms from the FoxPack and dumped it on the floor. He opened it and pulled out a short pole. Then he screwed a big round net on the end. The two pieces joined to make the FoxNet. It used to be an old butterfly net that belonged to the twins' great-grandfather.

'Give me a piggyback, Agent J.'

'Hurry!' gasped Mrs Seabert.

Bella had almost reached Charlie, who still hadn't moved.

Jordan lifted his brother onto his back and Harry swung the FoxNet at the same moment the python struck.

Snap! went its powerful jaws.

Missed!

Harry had scooped Charlie off the light a second before the snake got there.

But Bella wasn't giving up that easily. She opened her wide pink mouth again.

'Going down!' yelled Jordan, bending his knees.

Snap! went Bella's jaws.

Missed again!

Harry and Jordan landed in a heap on the floor. Charlie was safe in the FoxNet.

At least, Charlie *should* have been safe. But the FoxNet was ninety years old and was meant for catching butterflies, not cockatoos.

Rip!

The silk net fell apart and Charlie came flapping out.

'Catch him!' cried Harry.

Jordan made a grab for the panicked cockatoo, but it slipped through his fingers and flapped back up towards the ceiling, where Bella was waiting.

Mrs Seabert screamed a warning, but Charlie didn't listen.

Snap!

Jordan couldn't look. Poor Charlie had

become a python's breakfast for sure.

'Get back!' yelled an angry voice.

Jordan opened his eyes. Harry had climbed up on the stove and was fighting Bella off with the shredded FoxNet. But he was too late to save Charlie. A single white feather stuck out from one corner of the python's mouth.

Poor Charlie! Jordan thought.

'WHO'S A PRETTY BOY!'

Huh?

Looking up, Jordan saw more white feathers. They belonged to an upside-down cockatoo.

Charlie was alive!

Somehow the cockatoo had got away from Bella. He was clinging to the cover of a fan in the ceiling above the stove. Bella was trying to get him, but Harry kept pushing her back with the loop of wire on the end of the FoxNet's pole. But the wire was bending a little more each time the huge python struck at Charlie.

'Do something, Agent J,' gasped Harry. 'I can't hold Bella off much longer!'

Jordan felt helpless. Charlie was hanging from the ceiling nearly two metres above his head. How could he reach him?

'Shoo! Shoo!' he cried, waving his hands at the terrified bird.

It didn't work. Charlie's claws were locked onto the fan's plastic cover. He was too scared to move.

'Pet Whisperer!' yelled his brother.

Jordan was surprised to hear his old superhero name. When they were little, he used to think he could send messages to pets. It started when Myrtle was a puppy. If he closed his eyes and really concentrated, sometimes Jordan could make Myrtle do things without talking. It was like speaking in thoughts. Sometimes it seemed to work with their guinea pigs too.

That was years ago. Jordan was too old for pretend games now.

But it was Charlie's only chance.

Jordan put his arms down and closed his eyes. Think like a cockatoo, he told himself.

But something bumped into him, spoiling his concentration. It was Mrs Seabert, waving a broom. She poked the bristly end up towards the cockatoo.

'Jump on this, Charlie,' she said.

Charlie didn't move. He was frozen in fear.

Just then, Bella made an extra powerful lunge, and nearly got past the bent FoxNet.

'Jordan, *hurry*!' yelped Harry.

They weren't supposed to say each other's real names in front of people, but this was an emergency.

Jordan closed his eyes and tried to make himself calm inside.

Come to me! he whispered in his mind, holding out his hands.

WHUMP, THUNK AND CRASH

WHUMP!

Something landed in Jordan's arms. It didn't feel like a cockatoo – it had fur, not feathers. He opened his eyes.

It was Mrs Seabert's cat! It must have jumped down off the fridge because it saw him holding out his hands.

Or had the cat heard his mind-whisper?

There was no time to wonder because next moment . . .

THUNK!

Something else came crashing down.

It wasn't a cockatoo, either. It was the cover from the fan. The one Charlie had been clinging to.

Uh-oh!

Jordan looked up. There was a round hole where the fan had been. The broken fan dangled on some green and red wires above Jordan's head.

Charlie was flying around the room screeching.

Mrs Seabert went after him, trying to get him to land on the broom. But she was just making things worse. The cockatoo thought the big bristly broom was chasing him. He nearly flew straight into Bella.

Snap! went the python's jaws.

This time she didn't get just one feather, she got a whole mouthful. But Harry beat her back with the FoxNet's handle before she could take another bite.

Screech! Charlie flew one more lap around the kitchen, scattering loose feathers behind him like large snowflakes. Then he flapped up through the hole and disappeared into the ceiling.

'Oh my goodness!' wailed Mrs Seabert. 'My poor boy!'

'It's okay, Mrs Seabert,' said Harry, jumping down off the stove. 'At least he's safe from Bella up there.'

But Harry was wrong.

'Agent H, look!' Jordan cried.

Bella had stretched across from the top of the cupboards to the hole where Charlie had disappeared. Some of her was already in the ceiling.

Now that he was back on the floor, Harry could no longer reach her with the bent FoxNet. But as more of Bella's long scaly body slid into the hole, her tail slipped off the cupboards and swung down like a jungle vine.

Harry jumped up and grabbed her tail. His feet were off the ground. Swinging back and forward, he tried to pull her down. But Bella was very strong.

Slowly, Harry started going up towards the hole!

'Help me, Agent J!' he cried.

Jordan passed the cat to Mrs Seabert. 'You'd better take it out of here,' he said. 'Agent M's getting a bit excited.'

It was true. Myrtle was watching the cat and drooling.

Mrs Seabert raced away with the cat while Jordan turned to help his brother. He wrapped his hands around Harry's leg and pulled.

It was a tug-of-war, and Mission Fox was winning! The snake started to come backwards out of the ceiling, like toothpaste coming out of a tube.

But Bella's tail wasn't soft and squishy like toothpaste. It was hard and slippery and difficult to hang onto. Harry's fingers began to lose their grip.

Then they let go . . .

CRASH!

7

CAPTAIN AMAZING

Harry and Jordan landed in a tangle of legs and arms in the middle of Mrs Seabert's kitchen floor.

'Shishkebab!' cried Harry, watching the skinny end of Bella's tail disappear into the hole.

Jordan sat up and rubbed his eyes. They were starting to itch. And there was a tight feeling in his throat. He was allergic to cats. They made his eyes sore and gave him asthma. It was a bit of a problem for an animal rescuer.

'Where's the FoxPack?' he asked. 'I need my inhaler.'

Harry found the inhaler and gave him a puff. Myrtle gave his face a good licking.

'Thanks guys,' Jordan said. 'I'm feeling better now.'

Mrs Seabert came back into the kitchen without the cat.

'Where's Bella?' she asked.

Harry pointed at the hole. 'Up there,' he said.

There was a terrified **screech** from somewhere in the roof, followed by the sound of flapping wings.

'Poor Charlie!' Mrs Seabert said.

They all looked up at the hole. It was too small for a person to fit through – even a little one. Jordan was relieved.

'Is there another way to get into the roof, Mrs Seabert?' Harry asked.

'There's a trapdoor in the laundry,' she said. 'But I really don't think it's safe for you boys to go up there.'

Harry thrust his chest out. When he was little, he used to play made-up games, too. He pretended to be a superhero called Captain Amazing. Captain Amazing wasn't scared of anything – a bit like Harry, really.

'It's our *job* to go up there, Mrs Seabert,' he said in a deep superhero voice.

SCALES

Mrs Seabert led them to the laundry. The trapdoor was in the middle of the ceiling. It had a ladder that pulled down on a string. Harry went up first. He stuck his head through the opening.

'It sure is dark up here,' he said.

Jordan rummaged in the FoxPack until he found the FoxTorch. He climbed up the ladder and gave it to his brother. Harry shone it around inside the roof.

'I can see eyes,' he said.

The ladder had twelve steps. Harry was standing on step number eight. His head and shoulders were inside the roof. Jordan clung tightly to the ladder below him. He was only on step three, but that felt high enough. His knuckles were white from holding on so hard. He wanted to go back down.

'Do they look like cockatoo eyes?' he asked hopefully.

'Can't tell,' said Harry. 'I'll have to go and look.'

His GoFaster sneakers went further up the ladder – step nine, step ten, step eleven, step twelve. Then they disappeared.

Now it was Jordan's turn. He climbed up slowly until his head was inside the roof. It was dark and spooky. He could see his brother crawling away from him.

The dull light of the FoxTorch made long shadows on all the wooden beams, which looked like the bars of a jungle gym. There were sagging spider webs with sawdust on them. Everything seemed to wobble and change shape as the FoxTorch moved.

'Where are the eyes?' Jordan asked.

'Right in front of me,' Harry said. 'Can't you see them?'

'You must be in the way.'

Jordan stayed on the ladder. He was backup. If Harry needed anything from the FoxPack, Jordan could climb down and get it.

Just then there was a scuffling noise. A huge black shape came flying towards Jordan.

It looked like a giant bat!

'Grab him!' yelled Harry, swinging the FoxTorch around.

Caught in the light, the flying thing

changed from black to white. It no longer looked like a bat.

It looked like a cockatoo!

Jordan made a wild grab for it and nearly fell off the ladder.

Missed!

The big white shape flew off into the darkness on the other side of him.

'What's happening?' Mrs Seabert called up from below.

'It was Charlie,' Jordan called. 'I nearly got him.'

'We need something to catch him in,' said Harry.

That gave Jordan an idea. 'Mrs Seabert, can I have an old towel or something?'

She fetched one and passed it up.

'Agent H!' Jordan called. 'Here's a towel. Throw it over Charlie next time you get close to him.'

'You were the one who got close to him.' Harry's voice came out of the darkness.

Jordan could no longer see his brother. 'Why did you turn the FoxTorch off?' he asked.

'I didn't,' Harry said. 'I bumped it on something and it stopped working.'

'Can you fix it?' asked Jordan.

'I'm trying,' said Harry. There was a clicking sound. 'I think it's broken.'

Jordan looked down the ladder. 'Do you have a torch we could borrow please, Mrs Seabert?'

She brought him another torch. It was a big old-fashioned one, as bright as a laser.

'Look what I've got!' Jordan said, shining it through the shadowy roof space towards his brother.

Harry covered his eyes. 'Turn it the other way!' he growled. 'You're blinding me!'

'Sorry,' said Jordan. He swung the torch away from Harry, and his heart gave a big jump in his chest, like a wallaby was in there.

There was a large wooden beam right next to him with something coiled around it. Something that looked like one of those huge ropes they use to tie up ships.

Except it had scales.

9

PETRIFIED!

Jordan couldn't move. Well, actually he was moving – his arms and legs were jittering, his teeth were rattling, and butterflies were zooming around in his stomach. Now he knew how Charlie must have felt when he was hanging from Mrs Seabert's ceiling and Bella was coming after him.

Petrified!

Luckily Bella wasn't coming after Jordan. The python's long body was winding slowly around the beam like a fire hose uncurling.

Her other end – the end with the head on it – was slithering off into the darkness away from him.

It was going the same way Charlie had gone.

Uh-oh!

Jordan took a big breath and shone the torch past Bella. It lit up something white.

'Come quickly, Agent H!' Jordan called over his shoulder. 'Bella's here. And she's going after Charlie!'

'I'm on my way,' Harry said.

Jordan was still standing on the ladder, half in the roof and half out. He kept the torch trained on the cockatoo.

Move, Charlie! he mind-whispered. ***Fly away! Bella's coming to get you!***

But Charlie didn't move. He was frozen

in fear. And the python was getting closer and closer every second.

'You'd better hurry, Agent H!' Jordan called nervously.

'I'm trying!' cried his brother. 'But my shirt's stuck on something!'

Jordan swung the torch. Harry was about four metres away, stuck in a small gap between three beams. He was trying to unhook his MF T-shirt from a big rusty nail.

'Harry, you've got to do something!' Jordan cried. 'Bella's nearly there!'

'*You* do something!' his twin brother said. 'You're not stuck on a nail. And you're much closer than me, anyway.'

Jordan took another big breath. Harry was right. The only person who could rescue Charlie was Jordan.

Or the Pet Whisperer.

Can I talk to snakes? he thought.

But it was too late to find out. He couldn't become the Pet Whisperer in only a few seconds.

It took lots of concentration. He had to be calm. But his heart was racing. His thoughts were jumbled. He *wasn't* calm!

The Pet Whisperer couldn't help Charlie. Jordan had to do it himself.

Gulp!

10

A BITE OF COCKATOO

Jordan crawled all the way up into the ceiling. As soon as his feet left the ladder, he started shaking again. He couldn't help it. The tight feeling in his throat and chest was coming back. But there wasn't time to worry about it.

'Mission Fox to the rescue!' Jordan muttered to himself.

But who's going to rescue me? he wondered.

Bella stretched ahead of him in a long, wavy line. Her body slid away like a slow, scaly train.

Jordan crawled after her on his hands and knees. He tried not to think about the spider webs that brushed across his face. He tried not to think about his asthma, which was getting much worse.

He had to save Charlie.

Finally he caught up with Bella's tail. Then he didn't know what to do.

Should he grab it?

Jordan reached for the python's tail, but he couldn't make himself touch it.

Suddenly there was a blood-curdling **SCREEEEEEEEEEECH!**

Oh no! Jordan thought.

He flashed the torch beam along Bella's body until it got to the other end.

And there was Charlie – still alive . . . but not for long.

The python's head was raised. It was

about to take a bite of cockatoo.

Unless Jordan did something fast.

Here goes nothing! he thought.

He grabbed Bella's tail and gave it a pull.

SNAP! SNAP!

Snap! went Bella's jaws.

Missed!

Jordan had pulled her tail just as she snapped at Charlie. Bella's tail was joined to her body, which was joined to her head. So when Jordan pulled her tail, *all* of Bella went backwards. Away from Charlie – who was still frozen in terror – and *towards* Jordan.

Bella was a pet snake. She had probably been around humans all her life. She wouldn't usually bite them. But it was dark inside the roof. Something had grabbed her tail and pulled her away from a very nice breakfast. Bella was hungry. When she turned to see what was holding her back, all Bella saw was a dazzling round light. It must have looked like a huge bright eye.

The huge eye seemed to be getting in the way of her breakfast, so Bella opened her jaws lightning fast and attacked it.

Snap!

12

REALLY ALLERGIC

Jordan didn't see what happened next. It happened very fast.

And there was another reason he didn't see it. Just when Bella shot towards him with her mouth wide open, something

slammed into Jordan from behind. He dropped the torch.

Then there were lots of gasping and bumping and scuffling noises. It sounded like a fight. Jordan couldn't see anything because the torch had landed with its shiny end on the ground. He grabbed it and pointed it at the noise.

'Agent H!' he cried.

Harry had got himself off the nail and come to help. But now he was in trouble!

Harry was lying on his back, holding Bella's neck with both hands to keep her under control. But the rest of her was out of control. The enormous snake was coiled

around Harry in a big knot. It seemed to be getting tighter.

Jordan paused. His asthma had come back and his throat was getting so swollen it was hard to breathe. His eyes were sore, and there was a strange buzzing sound in his ears.

'What do you want me to do?' he asked.

'Wrap the towel around her head!' gasped Harry. 'It might calm her down.'

Jordan moved the torch beam. Mrs Seabert's towel lay next to his brother. Jordan tried to wrap it around Bella's big scaly head, but it kept falling off.

'Use both hands!' cried Harry.

'But I'm holding the torch.'

'Put the torch *down*!'

Jordan tried to balance the torch on a beam so its light would shine on them. But the torch wobbled and fell off. Jordan felt wobbly, too. He picked up the torch and tried again. His asthma was getting worse and the strange buzzing was growing louder.

Finally Jordan got the torch to balance. But he was shaking so badly it took him three tries to get the towel around Bella's head. Harry changed his grip on the python's neck to hold the towel in place.

'Now try to unwind me,' he gasped.

Gripping Bella's tail, Jordan tried to unwrap the huge snake from around his brother. It was nearly impossible. Bella was so strong! And Jordan hardly had any strength left. He needed his inhaler. But where was it?

'What's the matter?' Harry asked.

'Asthma attack,' Jordan croaked, still trying to free his brother.

The buzzing in his ears had become really loud. It was weird – he'd had lots of asthma attacks, but the buzzing noise was new. So were the yellow-and-black spots whizzing around his head.

'Yeeeow!' yelped Harry.

Jordan had to take a big wheezy breath before he could talk. 'What's wrong?'

'Something stung my leg!'

Jordon looked down and saw a large yellow-and-black insect crawling across Harry's ankle.

'Yikes!' he wailed. 'It's a wasp!'

'They're all around us!' cried Harry.

The buzzing Jordan had been hearing wasn't just in his head! It was real. Hundreds of yellow-and-black wasps buzzed all around them. They were European wasps – the very worst kind.

Uh-oh! thought Jordan. There was a European wasps' nest in Mrs Seabert's roof, and the boys' fight with the snake had disturbed them. The big buzzing

insects looked really mad.

One landed on Jordan's sneaker and tried to sting him through the sole.

'Get out of here, Jordan!' Harry cried. He was still tangled up with Bella and couldn't move. 'Save yourself!'

Jordan wasn't just allergic to cats. He was also allergic to wasp stings.

REALLY ALLERGIC!

One sting and he'd be dead.

13

ALL OVER IN SECONDS

Jordan didn't take his brother's advice. He had read all about European wasps on BRAIN. If he tried to get away, they would see him moving and go after him. They would get him in seconds.

Instead, Jordan sank slowly down next to Harry and the big knotted-up snake. He lay completely still.

'Try to...stay still,' he wheezed softly in Harry's ear. His asthma was so bad it was getting hard to talk. 'They're...going after...anything that...moves.'

MAIN
DESCRIPTION
HABITS
ORIGIN
OTHER INFO

The sting of the European wasp is very painful and can be dangerous. Unlike bees, which can only sting once, wasps can sting many times. They build their nests in gaps in walls or in roofs.

European Wasp _

Q W E R T Y U I O P   7 8 9
A S D F G H J K L del   4 5 6
Z X C V B N M ; ? /   1 2 3
aA @   space   ! ?   0 -

BRAIN

Bella's tail twitched. Three wasps landed on it and tried to sting her. Luckily for the snake, her scales were too thick.

'What will we do?' gasped Harry. He was having trouble breathing, too. Bella was wrapped around his chest, squeezing harder and harder. The towel had slipped

71

loose and he couldn't get it back in place.

Jordan looked towards the torch. If he could just turn it off, the wasps wouldn't be able to see them and might leave them alone. Then he could help Harry escape from Bella's coils. But the torch was too far away.

There's one other thing that might work, Jordan thought. It was their only hope.

As the cloud of deadly insects came closer, he made his thoughts go calm.

Leave us alone, he whispered in his mind.

Then everything went black.

14

PET WHISPERER

Harry's hand tugged at a loop of python tail that had been wrapped around the top half of Jordan's head. It was covering his eyes. That's why everything had gone black.

Then Harry's other hand held Jordan's inhaler to his mouth and gave him a puff.

'Breathe deeply, Agent J.'

Jordan did. It felt soooo good to be able to breathe again!

'Are you okay now?' asked Harry.

Jordan nodded. He was beginning

to feel better. 'Where did you find my inhaler?' he asked.

'It was in my pocket,' Harry said. 'I must have put it there after we used it in Mrs Seabert's kitchen.'

Jordan blinked up at him. 'Thanks, Agent H.'

'No worries, Agent J,' said Harry. 'Can you sit?'

Jordan slowly sat up.

'Where are the wasps?' he asked. 'And what happened to Bella?'

'A strange thing happened,' Harry said, rubbing his leg where the wasp had stung him. 'Suddenly the wasps just stopped attacking us and went zooming back into their nest. Then Bella just kind of relaxed and stopped squeezing me.'

'Cool!' said Jordan. 'They must have heard me. I told them to leave us alone.'

Harry shrugged, as if he didn't really believe Jordan could talk to animals.

'Whatever!' he said.

Harry started wriggling free from Bella's coils. She was still wrapped around him, but she wasn't squeezing any more.

'If you really want to be useful, Agent J', Harry said, 'give me a hand with this snake.'

15

FROZEN RATS

Harry was right about one thing. Once the towel was tied around Bella's head, she calmed down and was easier to handle.

Or was it because she had heard the Pet Whisperer?

Half carrying her, half dragging her, the twins moved Bella slowly through the roof like she was a big floppy rubber tube. But when they reached the trapdoor, there was a problem.

How could they get her down the ladder? They couldn't climb and carry her at the same time. She was too big and heavy. If they dragged her down, she might get hurt.

Jordan had an idea. 'What does Bella eat, Mrs Seabert?' he called.

The old lady was standing at the bottom of the ladder with Myrtle. 'My husband feeds her rats,' she said.

'Wicked!' said Harry.

Suddenly Jordan's idea didn't seem quite so good. Rats creeped him out – less than snakes, but more than bats and spiders.

'Does Bella squash them first, or does she eat them alive?' Harry asked.

'They're dead already,' Mrs Seabert explained. 'My husband buys them frozen from the pet shop and keeps them in the freezer.'

Harry's eyes lit up. 'You've got frozen

rats in your freezer, Mrs Seabert?'

'I'm afraid so,' she said, sounding sad.

'Awesome!'

Jordan climbed down the ladder, leaving Harry to look after Bella. Jordan felt sorry for Mrs Seabert. Frozen rats in the freezer. Gross! But it was better than live rats in there.

'Can you get one, please?' he asked.

Mrs Seabert shuffled to the kitchen. She was gone a long time. Finally she came back carrying a plastic bag with a white rat inside. Myrtle wagged her tail.

'It's not for you, Agent M,' Mrs Seabert said, handing the rat to Jordan.

'But it's not frozen,' he said.

'I defrosted it a bit in the microwave,' she explained. 'Bella doesn't like them too cold.'

Eeew! thought Jordan. He had to

take a couple of deep breaths before he could open the bag. Holding the dead rat by its long pink tail, he turned back to the ladder.

'Take the towel off Bella's head.'

Harry poked Bella's head down the ladder, then removed the towel.

Come and get it! Jordan whispered in his mind.

The hungry python locked her eyes on the dead rat and came rippling down the ladder, much faster than Jordan expected.

'Where's her cage, Mrs Seabert?' he asked, backing away quickly.

The old lady led him and Myrtle to a room at the back of the house. Bella played follow-the-leader, her eyes on the rat. It was a bit scary being followed by a huge, hungry snake. Jordan sighed with relief when he dropped the rat into the python's cage and Bella slid in after it. He closed the door and pushed the bolt into place.

'Mission accomplished, Mrs Seabert!' he said proudly.

But Mrs Seabert still looked worried.

'What about Charlie?' she asked.

16

REAL LIVE SECRET AGENTS

Rescuing Charlie was easy. Jordan stood on the ladder holding the torch, while Harry crawled back into the roof. He scrambled over to Charlie, being careful not to go too near the wasps' nest, and threw the towel over him. Charlie struggled a bit, but he settled down when Jordan closed his eyes and sent calming cockatoo thoughts in his direction.

Or maybe it was the towel that made him relax.

Two minutes later, Charlie was safely

back in his cage. He'd lost a few feathers, but he looked okay.

'WHO'S A PRETTY BOY?' he shrieked loudly.

Mrs Seabert fed him a cracker. Then she turned to the twins.

'What do I owe you, dears?'

'You don't owe us anything,' Harry said.

'But you saved Charlie's life! And you got Bella back into her cage. I must give you something!'

'We do it for the animals,' he said in his Captain Amazing voice. 'Not for money.'

'You see, we really like pets and animals and stuff,' Jordan explained, stroking Myrtle's ears. 'Someone's got to look after them when they get into trouble.'

'Well, if you won't let me pay you, at least let me give you a cup of hot chocolate and a big piece of cake.'

Jordan's mouth watered at the thought of it. He heard Harry's stomach rumble. They both looked at the clock above Mrs Seabert's fridge.

Even though it was Saturday, their mother would start to get suspicious if they hadn't come down for breakfast by nine o'clock.

'Actually, we'd better go, Mrs Seabert,' Harry said politely. 'Thanks anyway.'

It was Jordan's turn to wear the FoxPack. Harry grabbed Myrtle's lead. He was limping a little because of the wasp sting, so Mrs Seabert got him an ice block to stop it itching. Then she walked them to the front door.

'Thank you, Agent J and Agent H,' she said. 'You are the first real live secret agents I have ever met.'

Jordan looked at her to see if she was

joking, but her face was serious.

'I hope your husband gets better soon, Mrs Seabert,' he said.

She seemed confused. 'What do you mean?'

'You said he was at the hospital.'

'Oh my goodness!' laughed the old lady. 'My husband is at a hospital, but not because he's sick! He's a brain surgeon.'

Harry grinned. 'What's the difference between a brain surgeon and a chicken drumstick?'

'*Harry*!' hissed Jordan, nudging him in the ribs.

'It's all right,' Mrs Seabert said with a smile. 'I've heard *all* the brain surgeon jokes. Have you boys heard the one about the brain surgeon who donated his pet snake to the zoo?'

'No,' they said.

'Neither has my husband,' said the old lady. 'But I'm going to tell him all about it when he comes home this afternoon.'

17

NOT SPIDERS

As soon as the door closed, the twins gave each other an MF high ten (that's a high five when you count all the fingers).

'Mission complete!' they said together.

Myrtle barked.

'You did well, too, Agent M,' Harry said, giving her an MF high nine (five fingers and four dog toes).

She didn't really, Jordan thought. He had been trying to teach her *not* to chase cats. But maybe she did it to protect him. Maybe she knew Jordan was allergic to cats and shouldn't go near them.

Myrtle was always looking out for them. Even now she was giving Jordan a *really* worried look.

'It's okay, Myrtle,' he laughed. 'I'm fine!'

The dog whimpered. She tipped her head to one side.

'Stop looking at me like that!' said Jordan. 'You're making me –'

Suddenly he wasn't feeling fine. There was a creepy feeling on the back of his neck. It felt like . . . tarantula's feet!

Jordan froze.

'Harry!' he whispered. 'Something's on me!'

His brother's eyes grew big and he dropped the ice block Mrs Seabert had given him. 'Max!' he cried. 'How did you get here?'

Then Jordan remembered something.

He hadn't closed the lid of Max's tank after he'd answered the FoxPhone. Harry's big, furry tarantula must have crawled out and got into the FoxPack.

Now it was on Jordan's neck!

'Help!' he hissed.

'Don't worry,' Harry laughed. 'Max wouldn't hurt a fly.'

That wasn't true. Jordan had looked Max up on BRAIN.

'Just get him off me!'

MAIN
DESCRIPTION
HABITS
ORIGIN
OTHER INFO

The bite of an Australian tarantula is painful and can cause illness, nausea and vomiting.

Australian Tarantula _

BRAIN

Jordan stood very still while Harry got a stick and got Max to crawl onto it. As soon as the spider was off, Jordan backed away. But Harry couldn't help himself. He started following his brother, waving the spider on the stick.

It was a big mistake.

Myrtle thought Jordan was in danger. She snapped at Max. Harry jerked his hand away so Max wouldn't be eaten. The spider flew through the air and landed on the trunk of a tree. He scurried quickly up out of reach.

'Bummer!' said Harry, looking up at Max. 'Now we've got a Code Yellow rescue to do.'

Jordan thought it was a Code Red. 'Not me,' he said. 'I'm not rescuing anything.'

'But we're Mission Fox!' Harry's voice rose. 'We rescue pets, remember?'

Jordan folded his arms.

'We *don't* rescue spiders,' he said.

IS AN ANIMAL LOST OR IN DANGER?

MISSION FOX

IS ON THE CASE!

PANDA CHASE

Pingwu was huge and scary.
His big yellow teeth were as thick as Jordan's fingers.

When a truck tips over on the way to the zoo, Mission Fox
are on the case to track down Pingwu, the missing
Giant Panda. But when Myrtle tries to help, their panda
chase ends at the bottom of a water-filled quarry!
How will they get Pingwu out?

It looks like their *SOGGIEST* mission yet...

OUT NOW

Visit Justin D'Ath's website at www.justindath.com